Amelia

To Pheebe, Pifi, daughter, proud

Fred Weber

to the real Cookie

Amelia

by Fred Wehr

Illustrations by Rebecca Irish

The Nautical & Aviation Publishing Company of America
Baltimore, Maryland

ISBN: 1–877853–33–X

Printed in the United States of America

Library of Congress Card Number: 93–46451

Library of Congress Cataloging-in-Publication Data

Wehr, Fred, 1925 – Amelia / by Fred Wehr p. cm.
Summary: Using the goggles that mysteriously appear on her
seventh birthday, a young girl is able to experience flying in some
of her father's model planes and to meet Amelia Earhart.
ISBN 1-877853-33-X
[1. Airplanes — Fiction. 2. Air pilots — Fiction.
3. Earhart, Amelia, 1897-1937 — Fiction.]
I. Title. PZ7.W42415Am 1994 [Fic] — dc20

Cookie's Birthday Present

EPISODE ONE

Cookie's dream was fading. She was waking. The lady was gone.

Today was her birthday. She was seven. Beside her on the pillow was a package wrapped in silver paper and tied with a gold ribbon. She slid out of bed, picked up the package, and scuffed down the hall to her parents' bedroom. They were asleep. Cookie stood beside the bed and looked at them. Her mother opened her eyes. Sleeping mothers always know when a child is watching.

"Happy birthday, seven-year-old," said her mother. "That must be a present. Who is it from?" Cookie said she didn't know. "Sam," said Cookie's mother to her husband, who was just waking up. "Is this present from you?" He rolled over and looked the way fathers look when they want to sleep some more. "No," he said, and closed his eyes again. It was Saturday and he didn't have to go to work.

Then he remembered the birthday. He sat up in the bed, his hair down over his eyes. "Well, let's see what it is." Cookie pulled off the ribbon, peeled back the paper, and opened the box. Inside was a leather flying helmet like those the pilots wore in the old days. With it was a pair of goggles. Her mother and father looked at each other. "They're not from me," they both said at the same time.

Cookie put on the helmet. Her curls stuck out around the bottom. Then she put on the goggles and admired herself in the mirror. "Cookie," her father asked, "who do you think gave you those?" "Maybe it was the lady in my dream," Cookie suggested. "The pretty lady in my room. She said she looked just like me when she was seven. She was wearing a helmet and goggles, too. Her name was Melia."

Her parents looked at each other then back to their daughter. "Melia?" her father asked. Cookie nodded. "Could it have been Amelia?" Cookie nodded again, harder this time. "That was it," she said. "Amelia. The lady in my dream was Amelia. She gave me these for my birthday, I bet."

"I know what you're thinking," Sam said to Ellen. "But that present is not from me."

The Gee Bee

EPISODE TWO

The next day was rainy. Instead of raking leaves, which was what Cookie and her father were going to do, they spent most of the day in his den while he finished a model of an airplane he had been working on for several weeks.

Cookie stood beside him, being careful not to talk when he was painting thin stripes or doing something else that was hard. She was wearing her new flying helmet with the goggles pushed up on her forehead the way aviators sometimes did. Her father had told her that and so much more about airplanes that the boys and girls in her class thought he was a pilot. They didn't know the word "aviator," which is what Cookie and her father sometimes called people who flew airplanes. It's a word that's not used much any more.

The room was full of things about aviation. There were books on flying and pictures of famous planes and pilots. A big wooden propeller stood in a corner and reached almost to the ceiling. There were also models of airplanes that Cookie's father had made over the years since he was a boy, models of old biplanes that carried the mail across the country, of racing planes, of planes that had flown across the oceans in the early days, and planes from the armies and navies of the United States and other countries... England, France, Italy, Germany, and Japan. These and the racing planes were her favorites because they looked so fast and their colors were so bright. Some were silver all over, some blue and yellow, and one was orange and white with black stripes. Her favorite was dark green with yellow wings.

Cookie's father had a helmet and goggles, too. They weren't new like hers. They had been given to him when he was her age. Most of his friends had had them in those days, for boys then were fascinated by airplanes, and they wore their helmets and goggles when they rode their bicycles. But he had never flown an airplane, for he was very nearsighted. Without his glasses, he couldn't drive his car or read or make models.

By evening, the model her father had been making was finished. It was about as big as his hand, a fat little red and white racing plane with a big, round engine — Cookie knew they were called radial engines — and the number 11 on each side. Her father said it was called a Gee Bee, which stood for the Granville brothers who had designed it.

Now that it was finished and the paint was dry, Cookie asked if she could fly it. She meant could she run around the house with it, making noises like an engine. Most fathers who had worked so hard on something would have said no, even if gently. But she was careful with the models and hadn't broken one yet. Besides, her father knew how much she liked the things in his den, and he didn't want her to lose interest in airplanes. So he said yes, and off she went with the model in her hand.

Cookie flew the Gee Bee down the hall, downstairs to show it to her mother, then back upstairs to her own room. She stood in front of the mirror and thought about being an aviator herself, about flying the Gee Bee. She pulled her goggles down over her eyes.

Suddenly, she wasn't Cookie anymore. She was Captain Honey, a grown woman with blonde curls under her flying helmet. She was sitting in the tiny cockpit of the real Gee Bee at an airport in Cleveland, Ohio. It was a long time ago. The 1932 National Air Race for the Thompson Trophy was about to begin.

The race would be ten laps around a ten-mile course — 100 miles in all. Eight planes are on the starting line. With its huge engine, Honey's Gee Bee was the fastest, but it was also the most dangerous. She had flown it only once before, but that was enough to teach her that the power in that engine had to be handled very carefully and turns made very gently, or the airplane could flip over on its back. The pilot of an airplane designed by the Granville brothers had better be good.

The starting flag dropped, and the race was on. Captain Honey eased the throttle forward. Even at half-power, the roar of the engine hurt her ears. The airplanes to her right and left took off into the air. But not until Honey was certain her airplane was ready to fly straight and level did she pull back ever so gently on the control stick. The Gee Bee lifted from the runway. Only then did she move the throttle to full power.

Honey knew that the race could not be won by flying as the others were flying, close to the ground and hugging the pylons, which were the big towers that marked the corners of the race course. Her airplane was too tricky and dangerous, particularly in turns. She would make the most of the Gee Bee's huge engine and its speed. She would make her turns gently, well away from the

pylons and the other racers. She would travel farther, but she could fly faster — nearly 300 miles an hour. She would leave the inside of the race course to them; she would stay on the outside and win.

And that's just what she did. Leading all the others, Captain Honey flew the Gee Bee roaring past the waving flag that signaled the end of the race. She flew once more around the course — close to the ground this time — to give the spectators a good look at the winner. Then, very carefully, she lined up for her landing and touched the wheels to the runway. Even on the ground, the Gee Bee was hard to handle, for it wanted to veer off to the right or left, and Honey could not see straight ahead because of the big engine.

She rolled to a complete stop before turning around and taxiing to the judges' stand. There she leaned the fuel mixture to cut the engine, opened the little door in the right side, and climbed out with the help of her happy ground crew. Newspaper reporters and photographers crowded around, shouting questions, asking her to smile. She waved to the people in the grandstands and to the judges. Then she pushed her goggles up to her forehead.

She was Cookie again, standing alone in her room, a little girl with a red and white model in her hands. She crossed the hall to her father's den. He was cleaning his paint brushes. "Well," he asked, "how does she fly?" "She's fast," Cookie answered, "but very tricky. I don't think I'd fly her again."

He looked puzzled. Cookie handed him the model and headed for the kitchen. There was some cake left over from supper.

Flying the Mail

EPISODE THREE

The next night after supper, Cookie's mother and father washed the dishes and Cookie dried. Then her father went upstairs to his den to read. Cookie followed him. She had had her helmet and goggles on since she came home from school.

In the corner of the den was a big soft chair where her father sat when he read or just wanted to do nothing. Cookie's mother would put away the dishes and then read the morning newspaper because she could never find the time to read it earlier. Then she would come upstairs and tell her husband it was time to take their walk.

Cookie's mother had given him a book for Christmas about an aviator from France with a name Cookie couldn't say very well. Her father had been reading it for several evenings, and he picked it up now. "How do you say his name, Daddy?" she asked. "Saint-Exupéry. Antoine de Saint-Exupéry. He was a famous aviator and a famous writer, too. Remember the story we read called *The Little Prince*? Well, he wrote that and a lot more. This book is about him, and it tells about his days flying the airmail in Africa and South America." Cookie's father sometimes told her a little more than she could understand. But she remembered the story of the little prince. It had made her sad.

"Say his name again," she asked. "Saint-Exupéry. His friends called him Saint-Ex," he replied, saying the name like it was "Sanex." "He was flying the airmail when I was about your age. He died long ago. See that white biplane?" He pointed toward a model on the shelves. "Well, that's a Potez 25. A lot of them were made in France when Saint-Ex was young, and some of them were used to fly the mail. He flew the Potez and other French planes, too. In those days, flying the mail planes could be cold and dangerous work, and this book tells all about it."

On the globe of the world beside his chair, Cookie's father showed her France and Africa and South America. Of course, he showed her where she lived, too. Fathers always do that. He told her that French aviators explored the airmail routes from France to Africa and across the Atlantic Ocean to South America, and that they had to fly over the Andes, some of the highest mountains in the world. Then he showed her where they flew to carry the mail across South America. Most of their flights there were across a country called Argentina. When they flew over the mountains it

was to carry the mail to another country, Chile.

Cookie stood by the shelves looking at the model of the Potez. Except for the black letters on the sides, it was white all over. And it was a big airplane, bigger than any of the other biplane models on the shelf. "May I hold it, Daddy?" she asked. "Sure. But please be careful," he answered. As her father had taught her, Cookie held the Potez by the fuselage, the main part of the airplane, the part where the pilot sits. Then she lowered her goggles over her eyes.

In an instant, she was Captain Honey again. She was in a cold little shack with maps on the walls, standing in front of a table where a man sat with his head in his hands, studying some papers.

"Are you Monsieur Mermoz?" Captain Honey asked. For a moment, he continued with his papers. Then he looked up.

"I am," he said. "And you?" "I am Honey, Captain Honey. My French is not very good, I'm afraid."

He nodded. "You are Saint-Exupéry's friend. He told me you have flown the mail in the United States and that, like him, you have lived long enough to write about it. Now that Saint-Ex is ill, he has suggested that you fly his route for him. Is that correct?" Mr. Mermoz, who was the manager of the air service — the pilots called it The Line — did not waste words.

"That is correct, Monsieur. I have flown the mail back home, and I can fly the mail here. Your mountains are higher, but the Potez is a big strong airplane, stronger than our DH-4s. And I have many hours of night flying time. I'll get your mail across the Andes to Santiago or wherever it's needed."

Mr. Mermoz raised his eyebrows. "You have confidence, I see." He paused for a moment. "I'll be frank. As Saint-Ex has probably told you, his illness leaves me with no pilot to spare for tonight's Santiago flight. So, Captain, the flight and the mail and the Potez out on the field," he pointed out the window, "are yours. I hope that you are as good and lucky as your friend says you are."

Captain Honey saluted and walked out into the wind and the dust of the Argentine evening. Mr. Mermoz must have told the mechanics to make the Potez ready, for the engine was idling and the mail sacks were being loaded into the compartment behind the cockpit. Honey was wearing two sweaters and two pairs of wool socks. A mechanic helped her into the heavy flying suit and boots and then into the harness of the parachute that would be her seat cushion until she landed in Santiago.

She climbed into the cockpit, pulled on her big gloves, waved to the mechanics, and taxied down-wind, checking the engine gauges and flight instruments as she bounced along over the field. Then, turning into the wind, she pushed the throttle forward and began her takeoff run. In seconds, she was in the air, banking to the left, headed for the mountains barely visible in the west.

One hour later, the Potez was at 20,000 feet and it was night. Honey had never been higher or colder in her life. Here, the air was thin, and she was breathing faster. Overhead, a half moon shown down on the Andes, white where the snow lay on them, black in the shadows and on the rock outcroppings. To the right and the left, great peaks reached up above the Potez. She held the control stick between her knees and clapped the heavy gloves together to warm her hands. There were no lights at all on the ground below nor up ahead toward Santiago.

She listened to the engine as all pilots do at night over rough country. It was running smoothly. She wondered whether she was making good speed over the ground, whether headwinds were holding the Potez back. Saint-Ex had told her of winds so strong that once they held his airplane in place for half an hour before he could find a friendlier altitude. Her eyes returned again and again to the compass and to the fuel gauges. This was no country to be lost over or to have to land in, even in daylight. And if she did, how would anyone searching for her ever find a white airplane in all that snow?

The moon was in the western sky when the lights of Santiago came into view. The high Andes fell away to the right and left, and Honey eased back on the throttle, gradually descending into warmer and denser air. This mail, she said to herself, is going to get through.

Soon Honey spotted the rotating beacon of the Santiago airfield. Dropping to 500 feet, she made one pass over the hangars to check the windsock. It showed a light wind from the west. Some men waved up to her. Mr. Mermoz had told them by telegraph that a woman was flying the mail tonight. She would get a special welcome.

She climbed to the left and flew a wide turn to the downwind side of the field. The Potez was a delight to fly in the gentle air. She lined up for her touchdown, cut the throttle, raised the nose to shed speed, and touched both wheels and the tailskid to the grass in an easy three-point landing. Then she taxied to the shed where the ground crew waited.

Captain Honey cut the engine and pushed her goggles up to her forehead. She was Cookie, holding the model of the Potez 25 in her hand.

"We're going for our walk now, Cookie," said her mother. "Want to come along?" "Sure," she replied. Carefully, she returned the model to its place on the shelf. "You know what, Daddy?" Her father looked at her over his glasses. "Mr. Mermoz should have painted those airplanes orange."

The Saratoga

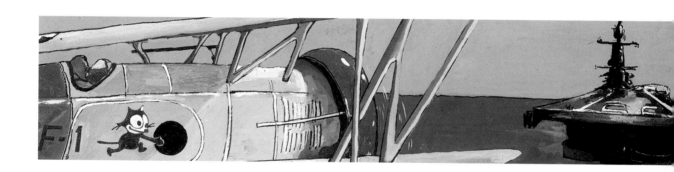

EPISODE FOUR

"Daddy, what's your favorite airplane?"

Cookie's father looked up from his book. "Oh, that's easy. It's the Boeing F4B-4. The F is for fighter, and the B is for Boeing, the company that built it. There's a model of it on the second shelf there. It's the little biplane with the yellow wings and the white tail. The white tail means that it flew from the *Saratoga*, one of the first aircraft carriers. This book tells all about it."

Cookie looked over her father's shoulder. He turned the pages. There were pictures of the *Saratoga*, a very big ship — he said they were called flattops by the sailors — made just for airplanes. It could carry more than 100 planes and was almost 900 feet long. There was a thing like a building in the middle off to one side. It was called the island, he said, and there was a wide black stripe on it. That was so the pilots could tell the *Saratoga* from the *Lexington*, another carrier that looked just like her. Ships were called "her," he explained. He had told Cookie that before. He told her lots of things twice, but she didn't mind.

One picture showed the *Saratoga* from the air. The flight deck — the deck the pilots took off from and landed on — was almost covered with airplanes. "These little planes up front are all F4B-4s. They are fighter planes. The next group are Curtiss scout planes. And these near the back — the stern — are Martin torpedo planes. Below the flight deck is the hangar deck. That's where the airplanes were stored. This picture was taken when I was about your age," her father added. He smiled at Cookie the way he did when he thought he had explained something so that she could understand.

Cookie studied the little model on the shelf. It was very pretty. Beside the yellow wings and white tail, it had a light grey fuselage with a red band around the middle. The engine had a red cover called a cowling, and there was a red V on the top wing and a number 1. On the side was a cartoon of Felix the Cat and the numbers 6 F 1.

"What are these numbers for?" she asked. He explained that the 6 was for the squadron, the F stood for fighter, and the 1 meant it was the first plane in the squadron, the squadron leader's airplane. Cookie decided not to try to remember all that.

She was curious about a hook under the fuselage just in front of the tailwheel. That, her father said, was the arrester hook. All carrier airplanes had them. When they were about to land, the pilots released the hooks which then hung down and caught one of several wires stretched across the deck. Without the landing wires, the planes would probably roll off the deck and into the water.

She was wearing her flying helmet with the goggles up on her forehead, and she had pulled the chin straps above her ears the way pilots sometimes did in the old days. Her mother liked that because it showed more of her curls. "Is it okay if I pick it up?" she asked. "Yes, but please be careful," he replied. Cookie lifted the F4B-4 from the shelf and pulled her goggles down over her eyes.

She was Captain Honey, leaning against a fence at the Naval Air Station in Pensacola, Florida with Lieutenants Silber and Chandlee. They are watching three bright new F4B-4s, that had just landed, taxi toward them. The fighters were fresh from the Boeing factory, and Honey and the other two pilots had been ordered to deliver them to the *Saratoga* to replace three older planes they would fly back to Pensacola.

The pilots from the factory parked the stubby little fighters by the fence, cut the engines, and climbed from the cockpits to the ground. The planes were marked for the first section of the squadron, red paint on their cowlings and the numbers 1, 2, and 3 on their sides. Each carried the Felix the Cat insignia of Fighter Squadron 6. The tails of all three were painted the *Saratoga's* white.

Honey and Lieutenants Silber and Chandlee chatted with the Boeing pilots, asked a few questions, and signed some papers. Mechanics filled the fuel tanks. In a few minutes, the F4B-4s were ready to fly. The operations officer gave Honey the carrier's position: she was in the Gulf of Mexico, 30 miles south of Pensacola. They would have no trouble finding her. Honey would fly the squadron leader's plane, number 1. She would lead the flight and land first.

They climbed into the cockpits, squirmed into their parachute harnesses, fastened their safety belts, and signaled the mechanics to start the engines. In a few minutes, they were at the downwind end of the runway ready for takeoff, Honey in the middle with numbers 2 and 3 to either side. She looked to the right and left then raised her hand and pointed straight ahead. The three little Boeings roared down the runway in a tight V formation, then leapt into the air and banked to the south.

Soon they crossed the beach and were out over the blue ocean. The *Saratoga* was clearly visible on the horizon.

As they neared the *Saratoga*, she turned into the wind, as carriers always do to prepare to recover aircraft. Honey pulled ahead, and the other two Boeings dropped into line behind her, spacing themselves so that their landings would be at safe intervals. She throttled back to lose altitude and then turned to the left so that the *Saratoga* was to her left and headed in the opposite direction.

Honey banked to the left again until she was looking straight down the carrier's flight deck. She leveled her wings and released her arrester hook. She could see the landing signal officer standing on his platform at the stern. From now until she was on the flight deck, he would be her guide. He would tell her by his signals whether she was "in the groove", or whether she was too high, too low, too far to the right, or too far to the left.

Honey's left hand was on the throttle, her right on the control stick. Her eyes were on the little figure with the red and yellow signaling paddles in his hands. His arms were out and level. Good. She was in the groove. The *Saratoga* loomed bigger and bigger. Now the signal — the paddle-across-the-throat signal — cut the throttle!

Instantly, Honey obeyed and then pulled the control stick all the way back. The little fighter reared. The hook caught a wire, and the wheels banged onto the deck. In seconds, crewmen were all around, unhooking the arrester gear and rolling the squadron leader's new F4B-4 out of the way of number 2, who was already in the groove and ready to make his own landing.

Honey cut her engine and the propeller came to a stop. Her plane was out of the way before number 2 caught a wire. Three was making his approach now. She looked up to the bridge and saw her friend Commander Todd, leader of Fighter Squadron 6. He waved and clapped his hands over his head, applauding her landing — she had caught the second wire — and thanking her for the safe delivery of his new fighter. She smiled and waved back. Then she pushed her goggles to her forehead.

Captain Honey was Cookie again. "I think you like that airplane as much as I do," her father said, looking at her over his glasses. "I wish I could have flown it." He looked a little sad. Cookie felt sorry for him. "I wish you could have, too," she said. "It's so much fun."

The Bush Pilot

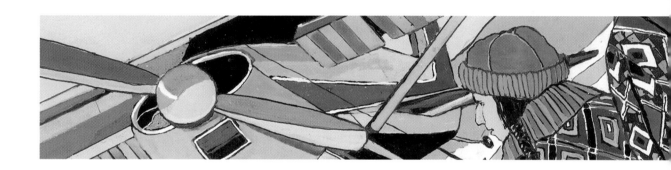

EPISODE FIVE

Cookie's father had been in Canada on business and came home just in time for dinner. "It was snowing when I left Toronto," he said. "I guess it won't be long before we get some down here, too."

"Can airplanes land on the snow?" Cookie asked. "Well," he answered, "if there's just a little bit, they can land without trouble. And take off, too. But when the snow gets deep, then they either have to plough the runways or remove the airplanes' wheels and replace them with skis. On small airplanes, that's what they do every winter in Canada. And Alaska, too. They need airplanes up there much more than we do, for there are not many roads. You've heard me talk about bush pilots, haven't you?" he asked. Cookie hadn't, but she didn't always pay attention. She shook her head. "I'll show you some pictures after we do the dishes," he promised.

Later, she and her father went upstairs to his den. "Now," her father said, "you asked about bush pilots." She hadn't, but she listened. He took a book from the shelves and leafed through the pages. "They are called bush pilots because they fly over the bush. That's what people up north call the woods. Here's one of the bush pilots' favorite airplanes. It's the Cessna 180 and it's fitted with skis. There are lots of Cessnas up north. Many of them — particularly in Canada and Alaska — never have wheels at all. They have pontoons in the summer when it's warm. Then they fly on and off water. When the lakes freeze, the pilots take off the pontoons and put on skis. With skis, they can land on the lakes or on the ground, as long as it's covered with snow."

"Have you ever made a model of the Cessna?" Cookie was looking over the planes on the shelves. "There's one I built last year up there on the top shelf," he replied, and stretched to get it. He placed it on his desk. It had one wing at the top of the fuselage — Cookie knew that made it a high-wing monoplane — and it had skis where the wheels would have been. The Cessna was yellow with red stripes down the sides. Maybe that was to make it easy to see on the snow, she thought. She remembered the all-white Potez.

Cookie was wearing her flying helmet with the goggles up on her forehead. She wore them a lot, even to school. Her mother had once said she looked like Melia somebody when she had them on. Was that the Melia in her dream, the Melia who had given them to her on her birthday? She had

asked. Her mother had glanced at her father and said maybe so. After that, they had been quiet for a while.

Cookie was thinking about the dream when her father asked if she thought she could fly a Cessna. "It's an easy one to fly, they tell me. There's one with wheels at the airport. I'll show you the next time we're out that way. Maybe you'll fly a 180 some day." Cookie had already thought about that. "May I hold it?" she asked. He nodded and didn't say anything about being careful. She picked it up and held it under the reading lamp. Then she lowered her goggles.

She was Captain Honey, sitting by a wood stove with her feet up on a chair. Corporal Mitchell, of the Royal Canadian Mounted Police, was at his desk, tuning his radio with one hand and pressing the earphones to his head with the other. Outside, the wind blew dry snow around the shack. Honey's yellow Cessna rocked in the tiedown ropes.

The corporal said something into the microphone and then looked toward her. "They've got four sick children up at Caribou Lake, and Mary Spotted Calf says they need a doctor fast. We can't send Doc Theobald. Bunky's flown him to North Bay to take care of Elizabeth's baby. But I've got my medicine kit and can help them if you can get me there. You know the country. What do you say?"

Honey got up and walked to the window. It was snowing but not hard, and the wind would be no big problem. She turned to Corporal Mitchell. "What did Mary say about the weather up there?" she asked. "From what she told me, it's like it is here," he replied. He waited for her answer.

She looked out the window again. It would be dark in two hours, but Caribou Lake was only an hour away — about 120 miles — and they should be able to make it with a little light left. She guessed that the base of the clouds was about 500 feet above the trees. A 500 foot ceiling wasn't much. And what was more, the clouds could settle to the ground anytime. "Well," she said, shrugging her shoulders, "I'm ready if you are."

Mitchell nodded and reached for his parka and mittens. Honey picked up the big can of motor oil that she had been keeping warm by the stove, grabbed her parka, and headed out the door. "Tell Mary we'll be there about four-thirty, and to put some of those red rags out on the ice. We'll need them if we're in cloud." The corporal nodded and leaned over the radio to call Caribou.

Honey was glad she had drained the Cessna's oil and kept it warm. In bitter cold weather, oil quickly becomes gummy, and starting an engine becomes almost impossible. She poured it back into the engine and then pulled the propeller around a few times to loosen the pistons. Remembering the red rags, she removed the door from the plane's left side. It would be very cold in the cabin, but with the door off she'd be able to look straight down when time came to land on the lake. Now she'd need her flying helmet and goggles.

Mitchell came out of the shack carrying the medicine bag and his blanket roll. He would be staying at Caribou for a few days until the doctor arrived. They untied the ropes, pushed the Cessna around to free the skis and head into the wind, and climbed aboard. Honey primed the engine, pumped the throttle a few times, flipped on the master switch, and twisted the magneto and starter key. The propeller turned and the engine caught. She let it idle for a minute.

They took off and flew low, 300 feet above the flat country, frozen ponds and forest below them. She would fly north to the third lake, turn and fly east for 12 minutes to Loon Lake, and then turn north again. With luck, she would hit the western end of Caribou Lake 20 minutes later. That's how we fly in this country when it's snowing, she thought. She didn't have to tell Corporal Mitchell what she was doing. He had been stationed in this part of Ontario for seven years and could fly himself — although probably not very well — if he had to.

Less than an hour after takeoff, they were flying along the south shore of Caribou Lake. They were lower now — 200 feet above the trees — for the overcast had dropped. Honey looked at the clock. Two minutes, give or take, to the village.

Suddenly they were in cloud. It was like being in a bottle of milk. White was everywhere. The trees below were gone, the horizon was gone. Was she still over the lake? Honey checked the clock. One minute to the village. Carefully, she dropped down another 50 feet. "Let's hope Mary remembered those red rags," she said. Mitchell nodded, but she didn't see him. She was looking out and down at what she hoped was the frozen surface of Caribou Lake.

Then there it was. A red rag. They were over the lake. No time for the textbook landing. Cut the throttle and drop the flaps. Upwind, downwind, or crosswind, Honey was going to land. Another rag. Good. They were still over the lake. But how high up — 50 feet? 25 feet? 10 feet? Honey pulled back on the wheel to raise the nose and drop the speed. Then swishhhhhh. They were on the ice. "Thank you, Mary Spotted Calf," she said.

There was a bump. The Cessna lurched to the left and then settled back on its skis. But the right wing was low. The ski on that side, Honey knew, had hit something in the ice and was damaged, maybe broken. The plane slid to a stop. She cut the engine, for in the fog she could see nothing except the airplane and the ice under it, and with a bad ski she couldn't taxi even if she had wanted to. Besides, the Chippewa would have heard them and would be running across the lake even now.

And there they were — Mary and Raymond Birdsong — standing under the left wing, looking very serious. Honey waved to them, and Corporal Mitchell opened the door, carrying his medicine bag. The right ski would have to be replaced. Looks like we'll be here for a few days, Honey thought. She pulled off her helmet and goggles.

She was Cookie again. She handed the model of the Cessna to her father. "Well, the children got their medicine," she said, and turned to look out the window. He smiled and shook his head. Wait until Ellen hears this, he thought.

Barnstorming

EPISODE SIX

Cookie and her friend Anne were sitting on the front steps when Cookie's father came home from work. Anne and Cookie were in second grade together. Cookie was wearing her helmet and goggles. Anne was wearing her baseball cap. They weren't being very friendly. Cookie had said the airplane towing the banner above the new mall was a biplane, and Anne had called it a two-winger. Cookie had said that's what biplane meant, and Anne had said Cookie was showing off.

"Daddy, isn't a plane with two wings called a biplane?" He put his briefcase down and hugged her. "Sure it is," he said. "Isn't it a two-winger, too?" It was Anne's turn. "It's a two-winger, too," he replied. Cookie knew he was just being nice to Anne.

Then she remembered the word her mother had used when they had called her outside to see the biplane. Her mother had said it looked like a barnstormer. "What's a barnstormer?" Cookie asked her father. She and Anne followed him into the house. "Haven't I told you about barnstorming?" he said. She shook her head. "Then I'll tell you at dinner, and you can tell Anne." Cookie was teaching Anne about airplanes. "Ellen, I'm home," her father called upstairs.

Later, he told her about the barnstormers. Many of them had been pilots during World War One. They flew around the country from town to town in biplanes they had bought from the government after the war. Because thousands of these planes had been built that the army didn't need any more, they were sold for very little — usually five or six hundred dollars. Many were Curtiss JN-4D's, called Jennies for short. They were slow, but they could fly in and out of small fields and pastures.

In those days, few people had ever seen an airplane, and they would pay five or ten dollars for a ride. That was a lot of money in the 1920s. The pilots were called barnstormers because actors who went from town to town putting on plays in barns had been called that, and it seemed a good word for the traveling pilots, too. "After we do the dishes, I'll show you a model of a Jenny if you'd like," he added.

The Jenny was dusty and not as good a model as most of the others. Her father had made it long ago when he was just beginning to care about airplanes, and he hadn't yet learned some of the tricks of good modeling. The tops of the wings and the fuselage and tail were greenish-brown — olive

drab, he called it. The bottoms of the wings were pale yellow. Barnstormers often painted their names on the sides of their planes, he said.

He handed her the model. "The front cockpit is wider than the back," she said. "Not on the real Jennies," he replied. "I think I made it wider on the model because I knew the barnstormers often took two people for a ride at the same time. I didn't know how they fitted them in. So I just painted a wider cockpit." Cookie nodded and lowered her goggles.

Captain Honey was thirsty and her water bottle was empty. The August sun beat down on the Jenny and on the woods and fields a thousand feet below. Off to her right was the Chesapeake Bay. She was barnstorming over the Eastern Shore of Maryland, looking for a few paying riders.

Up ahead was a town with a water tower. On the tank was the name Lewis. She was coming up on Lewis, Maryland, and she hoped somebody down there had never seen an airplane before. She throttled back and dropped down to buzz the main street. That should get their attention.

It did. People ran from their houses and stores, pointing up and waving. Honey grinned. There are customers here, she said to herself. She climbed to 500 feet and looked around for a place to land that was close enough for the people to walk to, but not so close that she would scare the children. And no cattle, either, Honey thought. She didn't like cattle around her airplane. Given half a chance, they'd lick the fabric right off the wings.

She dropped the Jenny into a field outside of town and taxied to a fence along the road where the people could easily find her. She cut the engine. Then climbing from the cockpit, she straightened her white silk scarf and brushed some dust from her new riding boots. Aviators have to look like aviators, she knew. She waited for customers. The boys always got there first.

But not this time. From the backyard of a house down the road, two little girls were running toward her. She had seen them playing in a sandbox as she was landing. A woman — their mother, Honey guessed — was running after them, calling to them. "Emily. Grace. You come here this minute. Do you hear me?" Emily and Grace kept on coming. Down the road from town came the boys. The men, who were just as excited as the boys, but slower, were right behind.

Emily and Grace got there first. Their mother was next. Then the boys and the men arrived, puffing from the run, circling the Jenny, pointing to the propeller, the tail skid, all the parts they could name, explaining, asking, laughing, beside themselves with excitement. Honey stepped from the lower wing and stood by the fuselage beside the big white letters spelling "Captain Honey" and began her pitch.

"Good afternoon, ladies and gentlemen, boys and girls of Lewis, Maryland. I'm Captain Honey and this is my Curtiss JN-4D, the famous Curtiss Jenny. I'm sure you boys know all about this ship, right?" The boys were flattered and they all nodded. Emily and Grace stood right in front of Honey, holding hands, not smiling, saying nothing. "Now I'll tell you what I'm going to do. I'm going to start that engine and climb into that cockpit and fly this airplane up there in the skies above your lovely town. And I'm going to look down on where you live, and over there to the Choptank River, and out to the Chesapeake Bay. And I want you to come along with me. I promise you the thrill of a lifetime. And it's yours for just five dollars. Now who's first?"

Emily and Grace held up their hands at the same time, faster than anyone. Honey smiled and looked toward their mother. "What do you say?" Then she paused for a moment, pretending to think. "I'll tell you what. Both Emily and Grace for five dollars, two for the price of one. And they'll remember this for the rest of their lives."

The mother hesitated and looked around her for advice. She got nothing but encouragement. "Let them go, Daisy." "Lloyd won't mind." "What's five bucks?" "Don't be a cheapskate, Lloyd." Lloyd was the father, who had just joined the crowd. He held up a five dollar bill and grinned. "Hold it till we get back, Mister," Honey said.

Honey climbed to the lower wing and put some cushions on the seat in the front cockpit so the children could see out. Then Lloyd held Emily up to Honey, who managed to get her over the cockpit combing and onto the seat. It wasn't easy, for she had to turn her sideways to get her under the upper wing. Next came Grace, who was littler and easier. Emily could see over the combing. Grace would have a hard time. Honey buckled their safety belt and set the engine controls in the rear cockpit. She showed two of the bigger boys how to hold the Jenny so it wouldn't roll until she was in the cockpit — it wasn't going to roll, but she knew the boys wanted to do something — and

walked around to the propeller.

She motioned the crowd back, said "contact" (that wasn't necessary either, but people liked it), put both hands on one of the propeller blades and pulled it down hard. The engine started. Usually it took several pulls. She ran around the plane, climbed into her cockpit, patted each little girl on the head, waved to the people, and taxied downwind. In a minute, Honey, Emily, and Grace were in the air.

The Jenny climbed and turned over the town. Emily's head was out in the wind, her hair streaming behind her. Little Grace could barely see out. Honey flew them past the water tower and then circled the town, first to the right for Emily's benefit, then to the left for Grace's. Each time she shouted, "There's your house. See your sandbox?" Then she flew toward Cambridge and the Choptank River. "Over there's the river and Cambridge. Ever been there?" She could see Emily's head nod. Grace was out of sight, probably looking at something in the cockpit. Children, Honey had learned, look at what they want to look at.

Honey tried to keep the rides to ten minutes. Emily and Grace had already had a little more. She turned back to the field, heading for a landing a safe distance from the crowd which was now 30 or 40 people. Honey guessed there were seven or eight more customers down there. That would be 35 or 40 dollars, enough to hold her for a while.

She touched down easily and taxied over the pasture, the Jenny's wings rocking. Up ahead, the men shooed the boys out of her way. She spun the plane around and leaned the fuel mixture. The OX-5 engine coughed and stopped. Honey climbed from the cockpit. Lloyd was standing by the wing, all smiles. They lifted the little girls from their seat and placed them on the ground, side by side.

"Well, ladies, what do you think of that?" asked Captain Honey. Emily said, "Thank you for the ride." Grace said, "I have to go to the bathroom." Then they turned and ran to their very relieved mother. Honey laughed and asked Lloyd if she could trouble him for five dollars and a glass of water. Then she pushed up her goggles.

She was Cookie again. She handed the model of the Jenny back to her father. "I'm thirsty. I'm going to get a drink," she said and ran down the hall.

The Jungmeister

EPISODE SEVEN

"Yung-mice-ter. That's how you say it. It means Young Master in German. The people who fly them — there are still a few Jungmeisters left — say it's more fun than any other airplane ever made."

Cookie and her mother and father were in Washington D.C. They had been to the zoo and to the White House where the President lived. Now they were in the Smithsonian Air and Space Museum standing under a little red and white biplane which was hanging upside down from the ceiling. This Jungmeister, her father told her, had belonged to a man named Beverly Howard — his friends called him Bevo — and it had been brought to the United States from Germany aboard the dirigible *Hindenburg*. "Have I ever told you about the dirigibles?" he asked. Cookie said he hadn't.

They spent the rest of the day in the museum and drove home the next morning. In the back seat, Cookie crayoned in her new coloring book and looked at the pictures in the books her father had bought in the museum gift shop. "Why was the Jungmeister," she didn't say it right "hanging upside down?"

Her father reminded her it was Yung-mice-ter and said it could fly upside down and do other things that most other airplanes couldn't do — rolls, loops, hammerhead turns, tricks like that. He demonstrated with his right hand and drove with his left. "Jungmeisters can easily do three snap rolls in a row. Like this." With one finger he made three fast little circles in the air. "Watch the road, Sam," her mother said.

They were home by dark. After supper, Cookie took her bath. Later, she went to her father's den in her pajamas and bathrobe, wearing her helmet and goggles. She had worn them to the museum, of course. One of the guards had said, "Why here's Amelia Earhart!" Cookie had asked her mother if that was her Melia. "Maybe so," she had answered.

"Do we have a model of the Jungmeister?" Cookie asked. Her father noticed the "we." And Cookie had said the name right. "Yep, right there in front of you. It's not red and white like Bevo Howard's, but green and white. That's it. The one with the checkered tail. Wouldn't that be fun to fly?" Cookie wasn't so sure. "Don't things fall out when you fly upside down?" she asked. "They sure do," he replied. "So everything loose has to be taken out of the cockpit. The pilots wear parachutes

and extra safety belts, too. Flying aerobatic airplanes — they were called acrobatic airplanes when I was your age — is very tiring. Let me show you something. Here, sit in this chair."

Cookie sat. Her feet didn't touch the floor. "You weigh about 60 pounds, right? Now pretend you're sitting in the cockpit and you're doing a loop." She pretended. He did a loop with one hand. "You would weigh almost nothing up here at the top of the loop and about 150 pounds down here at the bottom. That's like weighing almost as much as I do. Think what that would feel like. It would hurt, wouldn't it?" She nodded. "Those weight changes are called G-forces, G for gravity. Some tricks will make the pilot weigh 1,000 pounds for a second or two. Is this too complicated?" She nodded again.

Cookie picked up the Jungmeister and flew it into her room, rolling it, looping it, making engine noises all the while. She sat on her bed and thought about Melia. Then she lowered her goggles.

She was Captain Honey, and she had just walked into the airport office. The phone rang. It was Bevo Howard calling from Beaumont, Texas. He had a problem. "I've had this ear infection and the doctor's got me on some medicine that makes me dizzy. He says it's not the medicine, it's the infection. Anyway, I'm scheduled to fly my Jungmeister in a show here Saturday, and I just can't do it. Can you fill in for me?" Bevo was an old friend. Honey said she'd be there.

She left Friday morning in her own green and white Jungmeister and spent the night with her cousin in Vicksburg, Mississippi. Early the next morning, she flew across Louisiana into Texas to Beaumont. Bevo was waiting for her in the airport office when she arrived. "You're good to do this, Honey. I'm afraid there's only $100 and gas money in it for you, but you'll be in good company. Harold Krier is here. So are Jack Poage and Ned Surratt. Harold's got a new plane," he pointed toward the hangar, "and Jack's flying that yellow Zlin. Elaine Eggleston will make a parachute jump to start things off."

Bevo motioned to a man standing in the office door. "Come on over, Jesse." Jesse came. "Jesse, this is Honey, and she's pinch-hitting for me today." Jesse was going to announce the show over the public address system. He would introduce the pilots to the crowd, which was already beginning to gather, and explain what they were doing while the show was going on. A good announcer will add a lot of excitement. "I'm going to leave you two alone so Honey can fill you in on her routine. I'll see you later." Bevo walked over to talk to Harold, who was working on his de Haviland Chipmunk.

Honey and Jesse went over her routine, Jesse taking notes so he could tell the spectators what Honey was going to do before she did it. He would make it sound dangerous, and it was, particularly when Honey flew upside down under a rope only 20 feet above the ground. After that, Honey explained, she'd do three snap rolls, a hammerhead turn, and then land. "Three snap rolls?" Jesse asked. Honey grinned and repeated, "Three snap rolls."

Then she found Bevo and explained what she needed. He shook his head when she explained the rope trick, but together they set about finding some volunteers, two long poles, some rope, and rags to tie to it so it would be easily visible to the crowd, and to Honey.

By the time they were ready, the show had begun. Elaine jumped from a Cessna high overhead. She delayed opening her parachute long enough to frighten the spectators. An American flag hung below her and red and blue smoke poured from canisters on her boots. She landed next to Jack's Zlin as he was taxiing for his takeoff.

Honey and Bevo rolled the Jungmeister to the gas pumps and added a few gallons to the tank…enough to be safe but no more than necessary. The lighter the airplane, the better it flies. Then they walked back to the announcer's platform where Jesse was explaining Jack's maneuvers to the crowd. Harold would fly next, then Ned, then Honey.

Honey was in her plane with the engine idling when Ned landed. He taxied to a stop and stood in his cockpit, waving both hands to the applauding crowd. His performance was always popular, for he did all his stunts — the loops and rolls, the hammerhead turns and split S's — right over the runway where all but the littlest children could easily see him. Children can't see much at air shows unless they wiggle their way to the front row.

Now Jesse was introducing Captain Honey who, he announced, had flown in just that morning to pinch hit for "our old friend, South Carolina's own Beverly 'Bevo' Howard." Bevo, who was on the platform with Jesse, waved to the crowd and then pointed to Honey's Jungmeister taxiing toward the end of the runway.

When she was ready for her takeoff, Honey put on the brakes and pulled her safety harness as tight as she could. Then she waited for Jesse to wave his white flag, her signal to begin. He would have told the crowd that Captain Honey was the only woman Jungmeister pilot in the world and some other things that weren't quite true. And he would have told them, of course, that they were about to see what many aviators thought was the best aerobatic airplane ever made.

There was the flag. Honey pushed the throttle forward and the Jungmeister leapt ahead. In seconds, she was in air, flying level, three feet above the runway. Then, when the engine had given her all the speed it could, she pulled back on the stick and pointed the little plane straight up. She snap rolled, snap rolled again, then pushed the stick forward to fly level. That'll get their attention, she thought.

She banked to the left to stay in front of the crowd. Heading downwind now, she showed them a pair of slow rolls and then pulled the Jungmeister up into what looked like the start of a loop. But at the top, she rolled rightside up and flew upwind again. She glanced over the edge of the cockpit. Down below, the men were raising the long poles that held the rope and its fluttering rags. Now, the poles were up. Hold them steady, Honey said to herself, and keep that rope 20 feet above the ground.

Now she banked around to the right and, in a shallow dive, aimed her plane between the poles. Twenty feet from the runway, she flipped the Jungmeister onto its back and roared under the rope, the tip of the tail almost scraping the ground. Then one, two, three snap rolls, almost as fast as she could count.

Level and upright now, she flew downwind, her wheels almost touching the ground. At the end of the runway, she pulled back on the control stick and climbed straight up until the plane was hanging stationary in the air. There, she pivoted the Jungmeister in a hammerhead turn to the left and dropped, almost through the same air, toward the earth, then flared for her landing and touched the wheels to the runway where she had begun her takeoff roll minutes before. It had been a short but spectacular routine.

Honey taxied to the gas pumps, cut the engine, and released her safety harness. From his platform, Jesse was calling for her to take a bow. The crowd was whistling and clapping. She stood up in the

cockpit, waving right and left. Bevo was trotting toward her, all smiles. She smiled back and pushed her goggles to her forehead.

She was Cookie, sitting on her bed and wondering if she would ever see Melia again. Then she flew the little Jungmeister back to her father's den.

The Sparrowhawk

EPISODE EIGHT

The Forty-Niners were leading the Redskins 24 to 3 with four minutes left in the game. Cookie's father had lost interest, and her mother hadn't looked up from the Sunday newspaper for a long time. It was raining.

"Look, there's the Goodyear blimp." Cookie turned to look at the TV screen. The blimp was hovering over the stadium. "Do you know the difference between a blimp and a dirigible?" her father asked. "I think so," she replied. "If you let the gas out of a blimp, it goes all floppy. If you let the gas out of a dirigible, it doesn't. And dirigibles are much bigger, too."

Her father nodded. "Were much bigger," he said. "There haven't been any dirigibles since the 1930s. Sometimes they were called zeppelins or airships. After the *Hindenburg* burned up in 1937, the days of the dirigibles were over. There were still two or three left, but people were afraid to ride in them after the *Hindenburg* fire and they were scrapped a few years later."

Cookie guessed her father was going to show her something in his den, and she was right. "Come upstairs," he said. "There's something you should see." Her mother got up and turned on a movie. In his den, her father took a book from a shelf. It was about two of the Navy's big dirigibles — the Navy, he said, called them airships — named the *Akron* and the *Macon*. They were almost 800 feet long — much, much bigger than blimps — and they carried airplanes. Honey thought he was kidding until he showed her a picture of the *Macon* with a little biplane hanging underneath it. There had been eight of these planes, he said, each painted in its own colors. Only one was left. He reminded Cookie she had seen it in the Air and Space Museum in Washington. "The one with the funny-looking hook on top?", she asked. "That's the one," he said.

He showed her a model he had made of one of the *Macon's* planes. It had a green cowling and a green stripe around the fuselage. Like the real plane in the museum — they were Curtiss F9C-2s, called Sparrowhawks — it had a hook on the top in front of the cockpit. He explained that the pilot would climb down into his Sparrowhawk from the *Macon*, start the engine, release the hook and drop away. Then he would fly off to the right or left for maybe two hundred miles.

The pilot's job, he said, was to scout for ships from other countries so they couldn't sneak up on the United States Navy.

With a Sparrowhawk scouting out to each side of the *Macon*, they could cover a lot of ocean. The pilots had radios so that they could report anything they saw. When they returned, they flew up under the *Macon* and caught their hooks onto the trapeze they had unhooked from earlier. There was a picture of that in the book.

"What happened to the *Akron* and the *Macon*?", Cookie asked. Her father said the *Akron* had crashed into the Atlantic Ocean in a storm and that the *Macon* had crashed into the Pacific Ocean a few years later. They didn't burn like the *Hindenburg* did, he added. They just broke apart and sank. The *Hindenburg* was filled with hydrogen, which burns. The Navy's dirigibles had helium, which doesn't.

Cookie asked if she could hold the Sparrowhawk, and he handed it to her. She placed in on his desk and admired it. It was yellow and silver and light grey with the United States red, white, and blue insignia on the wings and the same colors in stripes on the tail. The green nose and stripe around the fuselage made it particularly pretty, she thought. Sparrowhawks were only 25 feet across, very small for a biplane. That was so they could fit inside the airships, her father said. And he added that they sometimes removed the landing gear so that they could fly faster and farther. After all, if you're not flying from the ground but from a dirigible, you don't need wheels. She hadn't thought of that. She lifted the little model and lowered her goggles.

The huge silver airship was pushing its way through rain squalls. When the sun broke through the clouds, the shadow of the USS *Macon* slid across the surface of the sea as if an enormous whale were just below the surface. They were 500 miles off the coast of California, and Captain Honey was in the control car. The commanding officer, Lieutenant Commander Herbert "Doc" Wiley, was letting her in on his plan.

"Honey, there are some admirals in Washington — and one or two up there in San Diego — who think the *Macon* is a waste of money and time. Well, we're going to show them something." He paused and a big grin spread over his face. Honey noticed that the crewmen at the rudder wheel and the elevator wheel were grinning, too. They must be in on this, Honey thought.

"Did you have a newspaper route when you were a kid?" the Captain asked. "No sir, but my brother did," she replied. "I folded the papers, and he delivered them." "Well," said the Captain, "beginning now, you're the paperboy — I mean papergirl. And you've got just one customer — the President of the United States."

She waited for an explanation, and Captain Wiley gave it. President Roosevelt was on vacation aboard the cruiser *Houston* on his way from Panama to Hawaii. Right now, the Captain said, the *Houston* and the *New Orleans*, steaming with her, were out there somewhere. He pointed to the southwest. "We're going to show the President what an airship can do. You're going to deliver his morning paper. Understood? Then shove off and carry out your orders." Airshipmen still talked like sailors sometimes.

Lieutenant Jennifer, the Executive Officer, handed Honey a waterproof bag containing a San Francisco newspaper and some magazines and gave her a compass heading and distance to the *Houston*. Carrying the bag, she trotted down the catwalk to the hangar. The aircrewmen had already transferred her Sparrowhawk from the storage trolley to the trapeze. Just the week before, its landing gear had been removed and an extra fuel tank hung in its place. "Who needs wheels when you're flying from a skyhook," the Captain had said.

Carefully, Honey lowered herself into the tiny cockpit and placed the bag on the floor. She squirmed into her parachute harness, fastened the safety belt, and made her check with the *Macon's* radiomen. Captain Wiley had said to keep in touch, and she planned to. It could be awfully lonely over the ocean with no one to talk to. The Sparrowhawk's little engine was idling. Honey glanced at the back of her left hand where she had written the course and distance to the *Houston*: heading 250 degrees, distance 110 miles. At her signal, the crew lowered her plane into launching position. She pushed the throttle forward, checked her engine gauges, and pulled the trapeze release. The Sparrowhawk dropped away and slipped off to the right, out from under the enormous silver airship.

The radio direction finder and the radio were working well. They didn't always. Honey was flying under the rain clouds where the horizon, except here and there, was visible in all directions. The *Macon* was no longer in sight. The *Houston* and the *New Orleans* should be up ahead and not far off.

Suddenly she saw them, steaming to the northwest about 20 miles away.

Without landing gear, the Sparrowhawk was fast. Within ten minutes, she was astern of the *Houston*. Had she been spotted? Maybe not. Anyway, she decided, let's buzz the President of the United States. Doc Wiley would approve. She lowered the nose and pushed the throttle forward. A few feet from the water, she leveled off and roared along the starboard side of the cruiser, then turned across her bow and climbed back to a position astern, watching the *Houston's* bridge for a sign of President Roosevelt. And there he was — she was certain — the figure in the old-fashioned boat cloak she had seen him wearing in photographs.

Now for the hard part. Throttle back, drop down, get the mail bag ready. She would fly the length of the ship as slowly as she dared and drop the mail on the deck. It wouldn't be easy, and it would take some luck. She balanced the bag on the cockpit combing. Now the *Houston's* stern was directly below. Now the seaplanes on the boat deck. Now the bridge. Drop it!

Honey pushed the throttle forward and climbed to the right, not yet daring to see if she had hit her target. At 300 feet, she leveled off and began an easy swing around the cruiser. On the bridge, a group of officers and sailors had gathered and were handling something. That's it! The President had his newspaper. And he was waving to her, too. She rocked her wings, then climbed away, headed for the *Macon*.

Soon, the airship was in sight. The rain clouds had moved on, and the *Macon* shone like a beacon in the afternoon sunlight. By radio, Honey had reported to Captain Wiley, "The President has his paper. Now he wants his coffee." He would like that. She was astern of the *Macon* now, ready for the hook-on. Throttling back and raising the Sparrowhawk's green nose, she slid under the massive silver shape so close overhead. Carefully, she eased her plane up to the trapeze. The guide bar made contact and the hook snapped shut. Honey was home. She pulled the throttle back and raised her goggles to her forehead.

She was Cookie again with the little model in her hand. "Daddy," she said. He looked up from the dirigible book. "This model isn't painted right for the *Macon*. The tail should be black." He nodded. She was right.

Amelia

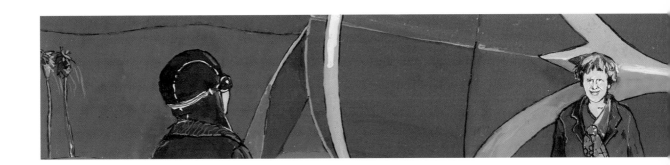

EPISODE NINE

"Daddy, who is Melia?" It was Saturday afternoon. Cookie and her father were watching an old movie about flying.

"Wasn't she the lady in your dream?" he replied. "Yes," she said. "But Mommy and the man at the museum say I look like Melia when I have my helmet on, and they don't know my Melia. Is there another one?: He said there was. When the movie was over, they went up to the den.

Cookie's helmet and goggles were still a mystery to Sam. Many times, he had slipped them off her head when she had gone to sleep wearing them. They were almost new when she had taken them from their box on her birthday — they had become a little scruffy since then — but they were of an old style, one he had seen only in photographs. And the tag inside the helmet bore the name of a company that had been out of business for years. Ellen still believed he had given them to Cookie, and he had stopped trying to convince her that he hadn't.

In the den, he took a book about women fliers from the shelves. It was dusty. He hadn't looked at it for years. He opened it to the chapter about Amelia Earhart. There was a photograph of her in her early flying days. She was wearing Cookie's helmet and goggles. No, he said to himself, a helmet and goggles like Cookie's. The ear flaps were pulled up, too. And Amelia Earhart looked like Cookie grown up. He was astonished.

"What's the matter, Daddy?" She was looking at him with an expression he hadn't seen before. He showed her the picture. "Here's the other Melia. Her name was Amelia Earhart. She was a very famous woman pilot. Her friends called her A E." Cookie looked up at him. "That's my Melia," she said. He had expected that.

He told Cookie all he knew about Amelia Earhart. He told of her attempt to fly around the world in 1937 and how she and her navigator, Fred Noonan, were lost somewhere in the Pacific Ocean when their Lockheed Electra ran out of fuel. "Did she die?", Cookie asked. "I'm afraid so," he replied. Cookie left the room.

She and her father didn't say much at dinner. Sam hadn't told Ellen about the two Amelias. That would wait until their daughter was asleep. They did the dishes, and Ellen began to read the morn-

ing paper. Cookie wanted to hear more about her father's Amelia, so they went upstairs to the den.

"Here's the Lockheed Vega that Amelia Earhart flew from Hawaii to California two years before her last flight. I was about your age then. She was the first person ever to fly that route solo. That means alone. You knew that, didn't you?" Cookie nodded. From the top shelf, he had taken down a model of a red monoplane with gold trim. "Amelia called this her little red bus. It's in the Air and Space Museum in Washington now. The Vega was one of several Lockheed planes named for stars. It was fast in its time but, I understand, hard to handle on the ground. Look at the size of those wheels."

He handed her the model. It was a big airplane with a radial engine. The wheels were very big. Cookie knew that was so the plane could takeoff more easily from rough fields. The fuselage was round and the wings were thick. The pilot — Amelia — sat in a little cabin on top of the fuselage where the wings joined. She wouldn't have needed goggles in there.

Outside it was dark. Cookie walked to the window and looked out on her backyard. A full moon was rising. She looked back to her father. He was reading the book about women aviators. She lowered her goggles.

Captain Honey was talking with Paul Mantz, Amelia's good friend and business partner. They were at Wheeler Field near Honolulu, and Paul was complaining about the condition of the field. "With all that extra weight she's carrying, she'll have trouble getting the plane out of the mud." It had been raining hard and the ground was soggy. Amelia's red Vega was out on the tarmac. She was in the office with her husband George who, Paul told her, was nervous as a cat. "George is always nervous when A E is taking off on a flight like this."

Honey knew what Paul and only a few other people knew: Amelia was going to attempt a solo flight to California. Where she would land in California would depend on where she crossed the coast. Honey was betting on Oakland.

"Hi, Honey. What's new?" Amelia was walking toward them. Her husband, George Putnam, was with her, talking over his shoulder to someone Honey didn't know but suspected was a newspaper reporter. George always wanted plenty of publicity about his wife, but he wanted to keep the desti-

nation of this flight secret until she was off the ground. A E and George weren't at all alike, but they seemed to get along fine.

Honey gave Amelia a hug. "You're about ready, I guess," she said. Amelia smiled. "When Paul says go, I go. Right?" Paul smiled. George wasn't listening. He was telling the reporter something, but probably not much. Paul walked out to the Vega. He spoke to the mechanic who had just closed the engine cowling. Then he turned and shouted to Amelia, "Let's go." He motioned her to the plane.

Amelia kissed George goodbye — he was still talking to the reporter — and headed toward the red and gold airplane. Honey called to her. "Where are your helmet and goggles?" Amelia waved toward the plane. "Who needs them in a closed cockpit?" she asked. George had heard and saw Honey's point. Aviators have to look like aviators. "Honey's right. Where are they?" he asked. Amelia said they were back at the hotel and waved goodbye again. Honey ran after her. "A E," she insisted, "you've got to look the part. Take mine." And Honey snatched her helmet and goggles from her head.

Cookie was at the window looking at the moon. Ellen came into the room with a cup of coffee for Sam. The little girl turned to her parents, the model of the Vega in her hands. There were tears on her cheeks. "Weren't you just wearing your helmet and goggles?" her father asked. Cookie nodded. "I gave them back to Melia," she said.